For Edna Rose, who didn't get to find her colors
but made the world brighter anyway

A Penguin Story
Copyright © 2009 by Antoinette Portis

Manufactured in China.
Library of Congress Cataloging-in-Publication Data is available.
ISBN 978-0-06-145688-6 (trade bdg.) — ISBN 978-0-06-145689-3 (lib. bdg.)

Design by Antoinette Portis and Martha Rago
1 2 3 4 5 6 7 8 9 10 ❖ First Edition

Antoinette Portis

A Penguin Story

HarperCollins**Publishers**

White, thinks Edna. *Like yesterday.*

Black. Like tomorrow.

Blue, blue, blue. Forever.

"There is white ice for sliding," says Edna.
"There is black night for seeing stars.

There is blue sea for hunting fish.
But there must be something else."

"Edna," calls a little penguin, "come play with us!"

"I can't," she says. "I'm busy."

"Doing what?" ask the twins.

"Looking for something that's not white, not black, not blue."

"When you get tired of looking, come play," says the little penguin.

"Edna," calls a large penguin. "Come fish with me!"

"I can't," she says. "I'm busy."

"Doing what?"

"Looking for something."

"You mean something to eat?" he asks. "Like lunch?"

"No," says Edna. "Something else."

"When you get tired of looking, come fish," he says.

I'll never get tired of looking, thinks Edna.

The next day she sets off to find the something else.

The large penguin packs her a lunch.

She looks   and looks

and looks.

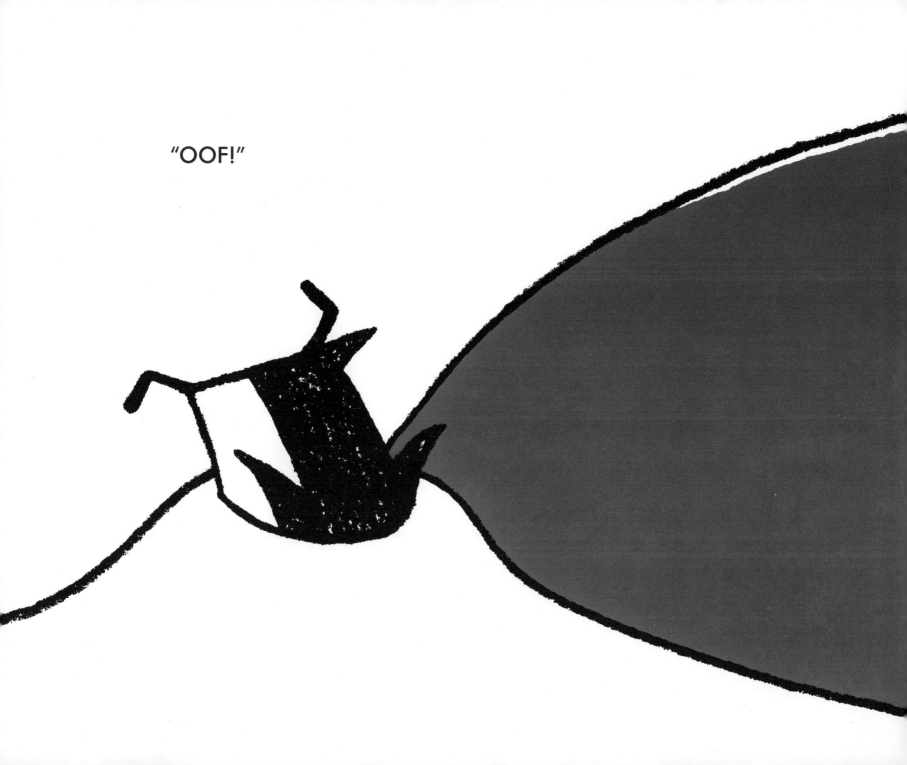

"WOW!"

"I knew it! The world isn't
only white, black, and blue!"

Edna runs home as fast as she can.
"I found the something else I was looking for!
Come and see!"

Everyone rushes off
without eating lunch.

Or dinner.

"Look!" says Edna.

"WOW!" say the penguins.

"This really *is* something else."

When the scientists pack up their camp,
Edna pitches in. It's the least she can do.

The large penguin looks for lunch.

The plane is ready to go.

Thanks for the something else, thinks Edna.

For the penguins, the way home seems short.

"Wow! Now we've got something that's not white," says Edna.

"Not black!" say the twins.

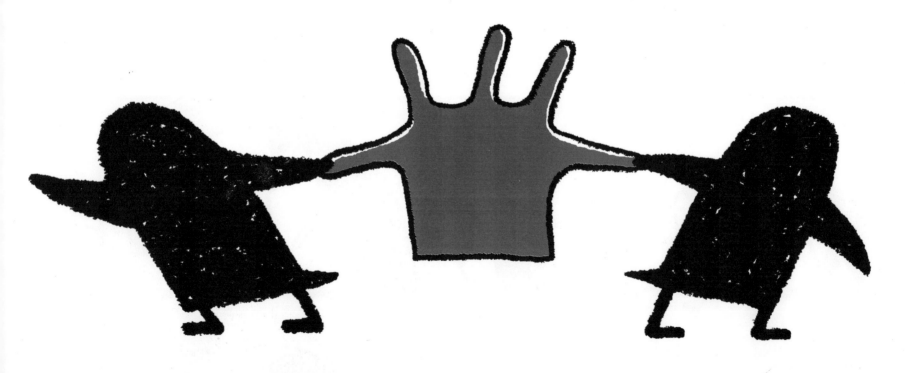

"Not blue!" says the little penguin.

"And definitely not lunch," says the large penguin.

The next day, Edna wonders,
What else could there be?

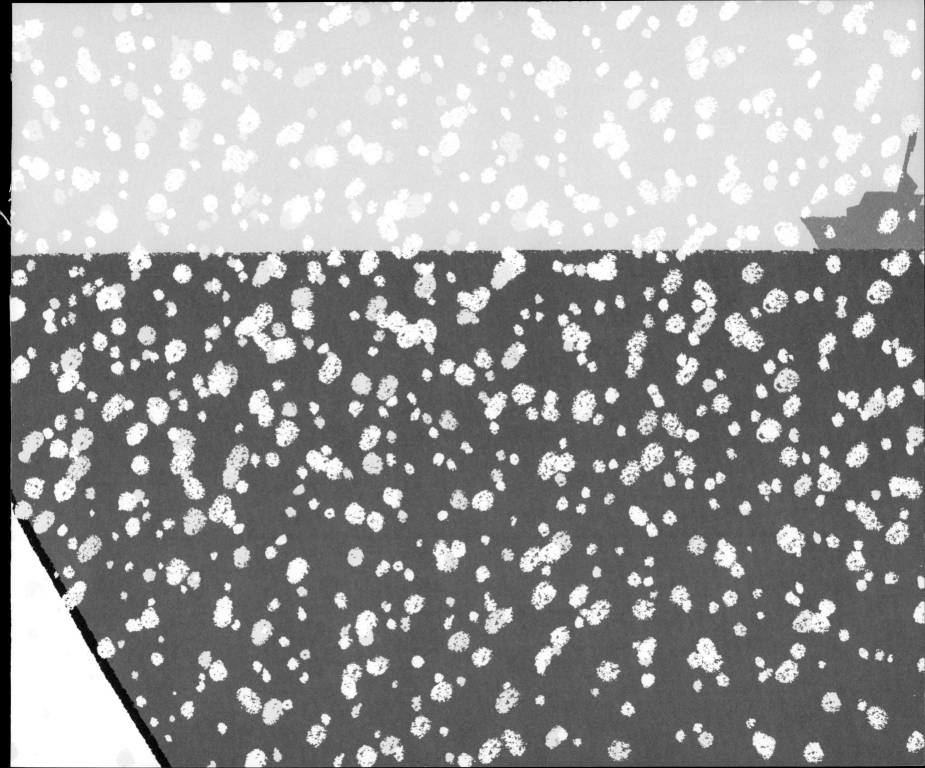